The EYE Stone

BRAD BORING

NEWMAN SPRINGS PUBLISHING
320 Broad Street
Red Bank, NJ 07701

First originally published by Newman Springs Publishing 2023

ISBN 979-8-88763-970-3 (Paperback)
ISBN 979-8-88763-971-0 (Digital)

Printed in the United States of America

Acknowledgments

The characters in this book are named after my parents. I would like to dedicate this book to my warm and loving parents, Tommy and Linda Boring. I love them with all my heart; they were the best parents a son could ever have.

My dad passed away on June 18, 2020, and I miss him very much.

My mom recently passed away on April 2, 2023, on a Palm Sunday, and I miss her very much as well.

I was brought up in a warm and loving family, and I've been blessed throughout my life.

Thank you, Mom and Dad. I love you, and I'm going to miss you both very, very much.

I would also like to thank my entire family and friends, especially Pam Watkins and Kay Still. Thank you so much.

May God bless us all.

Tommy and Linda Boring

INTRODUCTION

Major disasters happen all over the world. Technology is to help us in the future in case a disaster occurs. A team of scientists study all types of disasters.

Chief scientist Tom Highlander was working on a top-secret project. Working with Tom was his assistant, Linda Ordella, a highly qualified astronomer/technician, and two robots Tom constructed to assist in the project.

C-VOE, a conservation volecular unit is one of the robots programmed to detect tornados, earthquakes, hurricanes, and even minerals and gems beneath the Earth's surface.

R-CON, a radar-connecting unit, the other robot, is programmed to detect unusual encounters from the depths of space and other planetary readouts in the solar system.

Tom and his crew spent the last twelve years working to protect and save lives by detecting disasters weeks before they occur. However, when they encountered a phenomenon beyond their control, it was a race against time to save Planet Earth.

It was a cool autumn day. Two men were hiking through Stoneridge Point. As they walked along the rocky terrain, they heard a whistling sound getting closer and closer. They looked up as a ball of fire streaked across the sky, exploding as it hit the ground about two miles from where the two men stood. They were astonished by what they saw. They went to search the area where it hit but found nothing.

One of the men had a pocket telemonitor. He called the brigade squad and reported what they saw.

When the brigade squad arrived, they searched every square inch of the area but found nothing. The brigade commander thought the men were playing some sort of prank, so they called off the search. Two weeks later, many electrical storms hit the area as well as high temperatures were recorded, which were very unusual for this time of year.

On this dark and stormy night, as the thunder roared and lightning clashed all around the Bortex Space Laboratory, inside was chief scientist Tom Highlander who was working late on a *top-secret project.* Assisting him were his two robots R-CON and C-VOE.

And now our story begins.

"R-CON, contact Linda at the Planetology Space Station on your telemonitor." R-CON turned toward Tom as his telemonitor unfolded, and Linda appeared on the monitor screen.

"Hello, Tom, I was wondering when you would call," said Linda.

"Well, I need to check in with my assistant every now and then," replied Tom. "So how does it feel to be in outer space?" asked Tom.

"Well, for my first mission, it's turned out very well. We are installing the last solar magnetic energy panel, and the mission will be complete," replied Linda.

That's great, so when will you return from your mission?" asked Tom.

"We will be touching down at the Bortex Space Center in the morning. Will you be there?" asked Linda.

"Of course, I will, I wouldn't miss it for the world," replied Tom.

"Remember, Tom. We will be at landing Dock 2-B, and don't be late," ordered Linda.

"Don't worry. I'll be there," replied Tom.

"See you tomorrow," said Linda.

"See you tomorrow," replied Tom.

"Thank you, R-CON," said Tom.

Tom turned toward C-VOE who was receiving data from the main-circuit computer.

"C-VOE, are you scanning the area for a Burma ruby?" asked Tom.

"Yes, Mr. Highlander. I'm scanning the southeast area at Stoneridge Point," replied C-VOE.

Suddenly the scanner alarm went off, detecting a stone in the area as C-VOE went over to the digital map scanner that was projecting a three-dimensional hologram of the city. A glowing red dot was pinpointing the exact location.

"The map scanner detects a stone has been located in the Stoneridge area," said C-VOE.

"What kind of stone?" asked Tom.

"The map scanner indicates the type of stone is unknown," replied C-VOE.

"Unknown? Well, we need to check it out anyway." Tom walked over to the map scanner to check the stone's location.

"The *Orbiter Starship* will be landing at the Bortex Space Center tomorrow, and I need to be there when Linda gets off the starship. C-VOE, you and I will go search for the stone after I bring Linda back from the space center. She can stay here at the lab with R-CON," said Tom.

"Yes, Mr. Highlander," replied C-VOE.

"Well, it's getting late. I need to shut the power down so we can get a fresh start tomorrow," said Tom.

The next morning, Tom met Linda at the space center. She was walking down the hall as Tom walked up to greet her.

"Hey, Tom. You made it on time," said Linda.

"Well, I couldn't be late for an important occasion such as this now, could I?" replied Tom. "By the way did everything go as planned on the mission?" he asked.

"Everything went perfect," replied Linda.

"That's great," said Tom as they were walking out of the space center.

"So, Linda, how do you feel after being in space the last couple of months?" asked Tom.

"Well, I'm a little tired, but other than that I feel okay, but don't you think it's a little warm out here for this time of year?" asked Linda.

"Well, it may be a little warmer than usual, but you've been in space for the past couple of months. It may take a couple of days for your body temperature to regulate. Besides, outer space is much colder than it is here on Earth. Just give it some time," replied Tom.

"Well, maybe you're right," said Linda.

They got into Tom's air cruiser and drove away. After a short drive, they reached the laboratory and went inside. C-VOE greeted them at the lab entrance.

"Good morning, Mr. Highlander and Ms. Ordella," said C-VOE.

"Good morning, C-VOE," replied Tom and Linda.

"Well, where's R-CON?" asked Tom.

"He's replacing the servo module on the magnetic solar reactor," replied C-VOE.

"*Oh no!*" exclaimed Tom.

"Don't worry, Mr. Highlander. R-CON has everything under control.

Besides we need to go search for the stone," replied C-VOE.

"You're right. I guess we better go," said Tom.

"You guys go ahead. I can help R-CON work on the reactor. We should have it repaired by the time you guys get back," said Linda.

"Okay. We'll see you later," said Tom.

Tom and C-VOE walked out the door and got into the air cruiser. Linda watched from the entrance door as they drove away.

Tom and C-VOE headed for Stoneridge Point.

After being on the road for a while, Tom noticed a sign up ahead. "Look. Stoneridge Point. C-VOE, we're here. Now let's find that stone," said Tom. He and C-VOE got out of the air cruiser. "Okay, C-VOE. We'll need your sonar meter to locate the stone," said Tom.

"Yes, Mr. Highlander," replied C-VOE. C-VOE'S sonar meter was able to guide them in detecting stones and minerals beneath Earth's surface. "I'm getting a reading. The range is approximately two miles southeast from this point," said C-VOE.

"Good work. C-VOE. You lead the way," replied Tom. It was after a two-mile hike across the rocky terrane, when suddenly, C-VOE'S sonar meter went off, and its green light was flashing indicating something underground.

"Mr. Highlander, the sonar meter indicates the stone has been located at a depth of six feet right beneath us," said C-VOE.

"Okay, C-VOE. Let's hurry and get that stone because it's getting awfully warm out here," said Tom.

"Yes, Mr. Highlander. I will hurry," replied C-VOE. Tom stepped back as C-VOE started drilling. Tom was watching with anticipation. About twenty minutes later, C-VOE reached the stone as he retracted the drill, and extended his robotic claw to retrieve it. C-VOE carefully pulled the stone out of the ground and gave it to Tom.

"Wow," said Tom with excitement. "It was the largest red stone he had ever seen." Gazing upon it, he noticed something inside. "C-VOE, take a look at this. What do you see inside the stone?" he asked.

"There seems to be a flaw inside the stone, and it appears to be in the shape of an eye," replied C-VOE.

"That's what I thought. But what caused it?" asked Tom.

"Well, if my calculations are correct, this stone has experienced a tremendous amount of heat and then cooled very quickly, therefore cracking the stone from the inside creating a flaw inside the stone," replied C-VOE.

"But what would get the stone so hot to crack it?" asked Tom.

"I don't know. I will need to run some tests on it when we return to the lab," replied C-VOE.

"Well, we need to get back to the air cruiser before I melt. Linda was right. It's awfully warm for this time of the year," said Tom as they walked the two-mile journey back.

Tom and C-VOE finally made it back to the air cruiser. Once they get in, Tom immediately turned on the air conditioner. He looked over at C-VOE with a smile of relief on his face as he placed the stone in a secret compartment.

"There. It should be safe here until we arrive back at the lab," said Tom. He continued, "Well, we better get going," and he started the air cruiser, and they drove away.

On the drive back, C-VOE had been really quiet, so Tom asked him if something was wrong.

"Well, it's about the stone we found today. I scanned that same area two weeks ago, and no stones were detected," replied C-VOE.

"We've had a lot of rain the last couple of weeks that saturated the ground. It's possible the scanner was unable to detect the stone," said Tom.

"A stone that wasn't there in the beginning then suddenly appears two weeks later. Something's wrong," replied C-VOE.

Suddenly a call came over the air cruiser's telemonitor. Linda appeared on the monitor screen.

"Tom, you guys better get back to the lab quickly," said Linda frantically.

"Just calm down, Linda, and tell me what's wrong," asked Tom.

"All I can tell you is R-CON found something horribly wrong as he was scanning the planet's orbital patterns. Hurry, Tom. Please hurry!" said Linda.

"Linda, just stay calm. We're only five minutes away. We'll be right there.

Hang on, C-VOE. We need to get to the lab fast," said Tom.

Minutes later Tom and C-VOE arrived at the lab. Tom leaped out of the air cruiser and ran toward the entrance door and yelled, "Linda, R-CON, where are you"?

"We're over at the digital map scanner," replied Linda. Tom and C-VOE made it to the map scanner where Linda and R-CON were standing.

"Okay, now tell me what's wrong," asked Tom.

"R-CON was checking the planet's orbital patterns, and we are way off course!" said Linda.

"What do you mean way off course?" asked Tom.

"R-CON will show you on the map scanner. A three-dimensional hologram of the solar system shows all planets in perfect alignment except for one—Earth."

"R-CON is transmitting this *live* from the Planetology Space Station. As you can see, Earth was somehow knocked off its axis and is now heading directly toward the sun," said Linda.

"That's impossible. How could something like this happen?" asked Tom.

"I don't know!" said Linda bowing her face in her hands.

"Have you checked all of the computer data chips and the connector links?" asked Tom.

"Yes, Tom. we have double-checked the entire system network. Everything is working properly. I don't know what else to do," said Linda.

"We need to stay calm and figure this out, but first I'm notifying the brigade squad commander. R-CON, patch me through to Commander Riker," said Tom.

The commander appeared on the monitor screen.

"Tom, what can I do for you?" asked Commander Riker.

"Commander, I need you to dispatch all Troop Troller droids to evacuate the entire city to all underground shelters, and contact all US states and other countries around the world. This is a global evacuation commander," ordered Tom.

"Is this because of the record heat we've been having?" asked Commander Riker.

"Yes, we just want to keep all citizens safe from this record heat by sending them to the underground shelters," replied Tom.

"That's a good idea, Tom. The heat is even melting the ice and snow in Alaska and the Artic as well, and there is another thing that you need to know. A little over two weeks ago, before all this record heat, two hikers were at Stoneridge Point. They said they saw a ball of fire streaking across the sky exploding on impact about two miles from the checkpoint. We searched the entire area but found nothing. We thought they were playing some sort of prank, so we called off the search. I just thought you might want to know," said Commander Riker.

"Really? Well, thanks for the information," said Tom as the monitor went blank.

Tom sat there with a puzzled look on his face as Linda walked up to him.

"Tom, why didn't you tell him what's happening?" asked Linda.

"We need to keep this quiet for now. We don't need a huge panic on our hands. Besides I need to get more information about what we're dealing with here, and C-VOE and I need to run some tests on a stone we found today," said Tom.

"Oh, you found a stone? What kind?" asked Linda.

"The origin is unknown," said Tom.

"Well, that's odd," replied Linda.

"I know, but I want you and R-CON to keep a check on the planet's orbital patterns while C-VOE and I run some tests on the stone we found," said Tom.

"Okay, Tom," replied Linda.

Tom and C-VOE were in the test lab as C-VOE walked over, placed the stone inside the cryometric analyzer, and turned it on. A few moments later, a digital printout appeared on the monitor screen. "It says the origin is made of these gases: hydrogen, helium, calcium, sodium, magnesium, and iron. The most common element in the sun, known as a sunspot, originates from the sun," said C-VOE.

"The sun? You mean this stone came from the sun"? asked Tom.

"Yes, it originated as different types of gases bursting out from the sun creating a sunspot. Most retracted back to the sun. This one didn't as it kept going through space heading through a magnetic field before impacting Earth," replied C-VOE.

"Well, we know this is no ordinary stone. Now it all makes sense," said Tom.

"What do you mean, Mr. Highlander?" asked C-VOE.

"If this stone is a sunspot, then it is returning to the sun and taking us with it," replied Tom.

"This particular stone is not a gemstone. You might say it's one of a kind and extremely rare," said C-VOE.

"Well, it might be rare, and it might be the cause of our problem, and we need to check in with Linda and R-CON on scanning the orbital patterns, but first let's put the stone in the trio magnetic reactor," said Tom.

C-VOE walked over, placed the stone inside the magnetic reactor, closed the door, and turned it on. Suddenly the stone started giving off a bright-red glow creating a magnetic force knocking Tom and C-VOE across the room and slamming them against the wall. They couldn't move. The magnetic force was too powerful.

"C-VOE, you're right next to the magnetic reactor plug. Try pulling it out!" yelled Tom.

C-VOE moved his hand down against the wall and grabbed the plug, yanking it out and releasing the magnetic force, holding them as the stone's bright-red glow faded away.

"Wow, what was that?" asked Tom.

"It must have been a power surge activating the stone when I turned on the magnetic reactor. Apparently this is no ordinary stone," replied C-VOE.

"You're telling me this thing's alive? Well, at least we know what we're dealing with," said Tom.

Suddenly, Linda yelled out, "Tom, C-VOE, come quick!"

Tom and C-VOE quickly run out of the test lab to the map scanner.

"Linda, what's wrong"? asked Tom.

"Look. Earth's orbital speed has increased. Now we're moving faster toward the sun. What do we do now?" asked Linda.

"R-CON, check the original distance from Earth to the sun then check our current distance." R-CON displayed it on the monitor. "It reads the average distance from Earth to the sun is 91,500,000 to 94,500,000 miles away. The current distance shows about 74,800,000 miles and getting closer," said Tom.

"Well, it's time to get some answers as to what we're dealing with. R-CON, bring up Stoneridge Point on the 3D map scanner from about two and a half weeks ago," said Tom.

"What's bringing that up going to do?" asked Linda.

"Well, let's just say I have a hunch, and if I'm right, we may have found the answer to our problem," said Tom.

"Remember what the brigade commander said? About two and a half weeks ago, a couple of hikers saw a ball of fire streaking across the sky at Stoneridge Point exploding as it hits the same area we found that stone," said Tom.

"Well, let's take a look," replied Linda, as R-CON projected it on the 3D map scanner as they all watch closely. Suddenly a small ball of fire streaked across the sky exploding as it hits the exact place they found that stone.

"Good work, R-CON. The map scanner found it. Those hikers were telling the truth," said Tom.

"What do we do now?" asked Linda.

"Well, now we know that stone caused this whole mess," said Tom.

"How do you know that?" asked Linda.

"C-VOE and I witnessed the power of the stone in the test lab. When C-VOE put the stone in the magnetic reactor and turned it on, the stone started glowing a bright red with a magnetic force pushing us across the room and slamming us against the wall. Luckily C-VOE was able to unplug the reactor shutting it down," said Tom.

"You mean the stone has magnetic powers?" asked Linda.

"Yes, it is unbelievably powerful. C-VOE, go check the secret compartment in the air cruiser. See if there's any dirt we can analyze," said Tom.

"Yes, Mr. Highlander," replied C-VOE.

C-VOE came back with enough dirt to analyze, and he and Tom headed straight to the testing lab. C-VOE then place the dirt inside the cryometric analyzer and turned it on. A digital readout appeared on the monitor screen, revealing a very high magnetic content.

"C-VOE, now I know what happened. As the stone traveled through space, it went through a magnetic field magnetizing the stone, then crashing and magnetizing the entire Earth," explained Tom.

"What do we do now?" asked C-VOE.

"We need to go back to the 3D map scanner. I would like to try something," said Tom as they walked out to join Linda and R-CON at the map scanner.

"Tom, what are the results on the dirt?"

"The dirt has a very high magnetic content, meaning the entire Earth has been magnetized," said Tom.

"Is it permanent?" asked Linda.

"No, but this could actually be a good thing," replied Tom.

"How could Earth being magnetized be a good thing?" asked Linda.

"Well, it could give us an advantage for getting us out of this mess," said Tom.

"How?" asked Linda.

"Linda, I'm glad you asked. It's a long shot, but we've got to try it," replied Tom.

"You have a plan, don't you?" asked Linda.

"Well, like I said, it's a long shot, and there's no guarantee," replied Tom.

"Okay, Tom. Let's try it!" said Linda.

"R-CON, bring up the solar system on the 3D map scanner, and set the coordinance and directional pattern to guide Earth back into orbit," said Tom.

A green light appeared on the map scanner indicating all calculations were complete.

"Good work, R-CON. Now get me Captain Nolan at the Planetology Space Station," said Tom. Captain Nolan appeared on the monitor screen.

"Tom, what can I do for you?" asked Captain Nolan.

"Captain, you may find what I'm about to tell you hard to believe, and we're also going to need your help," said Tom.

Tom explained everything, and Captain Nolan was at a loss for words.

"Tom, will we be able to save Earth?" asked Captain Nolan.

"Captain, we're sure going to try, and with your help, we might have a chance," replied Tom. Now, Captain, we can't tell anyone else about this. It's just between us," he continued.

"I understand, Tom," replied Captain Nolan.

"Captain, I'm going to put you on standby while we get everything set up," said Tom.

"Okay, Tom," replied Captain Nolan.

"Linda, you and R-Con, stay here at the 3D map scanner and keep an eye on Earth's directional patterns. Let me know if anything changes," said Tom.

"Okay, Tom," replied Linda.

Tom and C-VOE stopped by the test lab to get the eye stone and magnetic reactor, transporting them over to the observatory. Tom and C-VOE reached the observatory and went inside.

"C-VOE, go ahead and plug in the magnetic reactor while I get everything set up," said Tom.

"Yes, Mr. Highlander," replied C-VOE.

Tom walked over to the master control center, flipped a switch opening the roof to the observatory, and switched on the magnetic guide transmitter setting the coordinance to the space station's magnetic energy panels, then switched on the telemonitor, and Linda appeared on the monitor screen.

"Tom, are you ready?" asked Linda.

"Yes, I'm ready" replied Tom.

"Captain Nolan, are you on standby?" asked Tom. Captain Nolan appeared on the monitor screen.

"Yes, Tom. We have the solar magnetic energy panels in place and ready to go," said Captain Nolan.

"Good. Okay, C-VOE, place the eye stone in the magnetic reactor. R-CON, set the directional coordinance to 1030. Everyone set. We've only got one shot at this. Let's make it count. Okay, C-VOE, turn on the magnetic reactor," said Tom.

C-VOE turned on the reactor activating the eye stone that gave off a bright red glow. When R-CON was transmitting the stone's magnetic wave to the space station's energy panel, a bright-red beam traveled toward the space station. Captain Nolan stood by as the bright-red beam bounced off the solar energy panels back toward Earth. Tom increased the diameter of the beam surrounding Earth with a bright-red glow.

"Okay, Captain. Reverse the solar panel's magnetic grid to full power," said Tom.

Captain Nolan reversed the magnetic grid to full power, but nothing happened. Earth was not moving back. "Tom, the map scanner shows we're not moving. Why are we not moving?" asked Linda franticly.

"Linda, we need to stay focused."

"Okay, Tom. You're right," she replied.

"Captain, do you see a boost switch for the magnetic panel grid?" asked Tom.

"Yes, Tom. I see it," replied Captain Nolan.

"Okay. Flip the switch," said Tom.

Captain Nolan flipped the switch, and several minutes went by.

"Linda, check the map scanner to see if we're moving," asked Tom.

"No, Tom. We're still not moving," said Linda.

"Okay, Linda, let's—"

"*Wait!* Yes, we're moving. We're moving!" shouted Linda interrupting Tom.

"That's great. There must have been a delay in the booster signal reaching us. I just hope the eye stone gives us enough power to get back into orbit," said Tom, and Earth moved back at a rapid speed. Several hours went by as the booster power's magnetic grid started pulling Earth back into orbit.

C-VOE noticed the eye stone's bright-red glow was fading fast.

"Mr. Highlander, look at the eye stone," said C-VOE.

"R-CON, give me the current distance of Earth to the sun," said Tom.

A digital readout came over the telemonitor screen. It read 93,000,000 miles as the 3D map scanner's green light was flashing indicating Earth was back in orbit, and the eye stone's bright-red glow faded completely.

"We did it! We did it!" yelled Tom and Linda with pure excitement.

"Thank you, Captain Nolan. We couldn't have done it without you," said Tom.

"My pleasure," replied Captain Nolan.

Not only did Tom and his team save Planet Earth. Remember the *top-secret project* Tom and his team were working on? Well, two weeks later, they finally found a Burma ruby completing the formula for creating artificial gravity for the Planetology Space Station.

Congratulations, team, for a *job well done*!

The end

About the Author

When I was twelve, in the seventh grade at Cleveland Junior High School, I was in a filmmaking class. All eight of us had to write a script so I wrote *The Eye Stone*. It was originally to be a horror film, but later I changed it to be a sci-fi story.

www.ingramcontent.com/pod-product-compliance
Lightning Source LLC
Chambersburg PA
CBHW072138150726
48002CB00004B/1532